SAVING HIM FROM ABSALOM

A woman's spiritual battle for her man oppressed and tormented by evil forces

ROCKSON RAPU

ISBN: 9798878128858

DISCLAIMER

DEDICATION

This book is dedicated to my God-fearing and diligent children, who have been incredibly supportive, enabling me to travel widely for facts and figures, and be able share some raw wisdom with their generation.

THANK YOU

This is just to say thank you for buying my book. Please endeavour to visit our website to download some free resource materials that will help you impact lives. Also follow us on Facebook, Instagram @rocksonrapu and subscribe to our YouTube channel.

Visit our website:

http://www.refinedresources.co.uk

SAVING HIM FROM ABSALOM

CONTENTS

ACKNOWLEDGMENTS

All glory belongs to God for blessing me with the necessary resources to write this book. I am especially thankful to our Lord Jesus Christ who fought all the battles for us and gave me and my brothers and sisters the opportunity to testify.

I thank God for "Kaye Dubayi, alias Pastor KD", who decided to make his story public. I am highly privileged to transform KD's story into fiction.

I appreciate the prayers of my brothers and sisters who have been praying for me.

Many people influenced my progress in writing this book, directly or indirectly. I want to honour these friends, relatives, and mentors for their invaluable support: Vishal Morjaria, Nosa Eweka, Emmanuel Egerton-Shyngle, Rev (Dr) ADT Gorton, Dr Tony Rapu, Apostle Sunny Odafe, Apostle Alph Lukau and Bishop Celeste Lukau and many more that I do not have enough space to mention here.

PREFACE

This book goes to the root of familiar mental health issues plaguing young adults today. It delves into a case of severe depression, phobias, and attempted suicide which nearly ruined a promising young man of God. It is the story of a young man who was good, handsome and intelligent but fell for the temptation of envy and bitterness. He wanted to be richer and more famous than his spiritual father and his biological father.

He pursued power the wrong way. Negative power corrupts and absolute power corrupts absolutely.

He went into severe depression and tried several times to commit suicide when the demons came after him.

His woman stood in the gap and prayed for him. She trusted God to bring him back and God did not disappoint. Her church was instrumental in offering spiritual and medical support through their in-house medical staff.

This story is a testimonial to the power of prayer and the miracles that God can perform in healing both visible and invisible health challenges. It is also a reminder that mental health problems do not have to be battled alone and that with the right support and faith, one can overcome any obstacle.

The woman's unwavering faith and love for her man, proved that true love can conquer all, and they are a living testimony to this fact.

These days, many young adults all over the world, especially in the UK are attempting suicide as a way of escaping mental health issues, without bothering about friends and relatives they would leave behind. The good news is that God is still in the business of healing and deliverance.

At the end of the story, the author proffered practical and biblical solutions to help those with similar challenges and to prevent such from happening in the future.

Few chapters were removed from this novel, to cut down on the graphics, and make it more family friendly.

The book was written in such a way that each chapter teaches us few life lessons. There is something to take away for both the fast reader who gets to the end of the book in no time, and the slow reader who digests the novel one chapter per day.

Please sit back, relax, and enjoy this story till the end.

Chapter One

At The Peak of Bleakness

It looked like there was no other way for Kaye Dubayi, alias Pastor KD, to go in search of peace, power and position in the body of Christ. He had been forced to contemplate going back 180 degrees to where it all began. He had been forced to think of going back to Ghana and Nigeria to seek help. It seemed his life was falling apart. From love life to spiritual life, things were falling apart. He believed that only the spiritual leader that initiated him into this Occult Church can help. He could not masquerade any more as a Pentecostal pastor or prophet. He had to do something very quickly before he loses his life.

In his desperation, he made a quick phone call to his bosom friend, Silas, to rub minds before making his plans to jet off to Nigeria to try to salvage his career as a "prophet". So many things were working against him. He literally had to watch his back all the time. Silas was ever ready to help. On the phone, he asked him. "Should I close down the Church and just disappear to Nigeria to start a new life? I am sure it won't cost me too much to obtain favour and the citizenship of that country, and procure a Nigerian passport in days rather than weeks." Silas laughed out loud. "Why will you do such a thing? See how many years you have invested in your Church! Everyone believes you are a genuine prophet. Even your newly adopted spiritual father believes you are genuinely anointed. Look at your congregation. Over a thousand members." KD replied, "My brother, see all the forces against me. Seven forces altogether! I am dealing with rebellion from close lieutenants in my Church. My woman is threatening to leave me, since I cannot sleep with her or marry her. My biggest sponsor wants his car back, and is threatening me with police. I am using a fake passport here and

Immigration will soon find out, if I am not very careful. One of my guys is into drugs and has been locked up. I am being asked to bail him out. My mother is seriously ill and I cannot even go to visit her because of immigration issues. The tax people are after me because of some discrepancies. I have been asked by the Chief priest in Ghana to deliver my woman for sacrifice so all these problems will vanish. I am so confused Silas! Sometimes I feel like committing suicide" He did not disclose to his friend one thing. That his life was in danger if he does not submit his much loved woman for sacrifice. That he will in fact be used as the sacrifice if he did not submit his woman. And there was a time limit. One month was the time given and he had used up one week pondering what to do. Now the clock was ticking, and KD was getting more confused and depressed.

There was a long silence. "Hello! Silas are you there?" "Yes I am." Replied Silas, "I am just thinking out a solution. I do not think that disappearing to Nigeria or committing suicide is the best option." He continued.

"By the way, have you discussed these issues with your spiritual father?" There was a longer silence this time. KD was about to break another bad news. "What nonsense spiritual father? I am done with all that rubbish. I don't believe in spiritual fatherism anymore. To hell with all the spiritual fathers, that only end up creating more problems in people's lives." Silas was shocked. He regretted in his heart that he had mentioned spiritual fathers. He became desperate to change the subject.

"What about deliverance prayers KD?" Silas now wanted to encourage his friend to go for deliverance prayers somewhere else. He had to do this without mentioning anything about spiritual fathers. He asked him. "KD, have you thought about deliverance in a big church where nobody will know you? Or you can contact one of the big Pastors under your Papa, for prayers." This was like adding insult to injury! "To hell with those Pastors who cannot even prophesy," replied KD. "All they are good at is wearing good clothes and overflowing regalia."

Silas quickly changed the subject, knowing that this line of discussion will only lead to more rancour and unnecessary arguments. Silas understands his friend to be a very stubborn guy. Sometimes the stubbornness is beneficial as it allows KD to pursue goals that others are afraid of venturing.

Silas then picked on Emily the sweetheart of KD, deliberately to say something nice about her and get him to cool down.

"Have you heard from your Queen recently?" KD usually refers to her as his Queen. Silas continues, "I understand she is travelling to Europe soon for business. I wanted her to buy some stuff for me."

KD felt a relief when he heard about his heartthrob. KD and Emily are not officially married, but they cohabited for a few years, in a way that enables them to be together over the weekends, before Emily returns to her home after the weekend. As a working class lady and a nominal Christian, she hardly prays, but believes strongly in God. She depends on her Church pastor to pray and prophesy into her life, every now and again. Talk about the way of an African woman with prophesy and prophets! Emily was prepared to destroy any relationships with family and friends, just to maintain a solid relationship with her Church pastor or prophet as some prefer to call him.

Emily loved KD especially because he was also very spiritual and believed in the power of positive energy and good vibes. Unfortunately, KD did not reveal his level of spirituality to Emily. He kept everything under wraps, fearing that Emily would leave him when she discovers the full length of his involvement in the power of the negative underworld or supernatural. The only person that he gave a clue about his spiritual escapades was his best friend, Silas. It was this same Silas he told about strange happenings each time he slept with Emily after joining the Cult. He had told Silas that he believed the unusual odour emanating from his girlfriend when they lie together in bed was a ploy by the spiritual marine wife and the chief priest to separate them.

After a while, Silas connected back to their mobile phone conversation, after the lines cut off, owing to network problems. Silas thought the problem was from the other end, so he called back to offer counsel to his best friend.

"KD what happened? The lines went off". "I thought it was network problems. I was seeing 'reconnecting' on my phone", replied KD.

Silas knows so much about Emily and KD he believes that things might be a bit different if Emily was let into the equation at this stage, to see what she can do. After all, Emily has a very senior pastor as her mentor in her church, who is capable of praying for KD from far, as distance is not a barrier when it comes to prayers. His plan is to find a way of convincing KD to open up to Emily. Silas doesn't want to be the one to reveal all the secrets. He cannot imagine himself doing so anyway. To begin the rescue mission he popped the question again, in a subtle manner. "KD, you know I have your interest at heart, and wish you all the best. Now I have been pondering this matter ever before you called. Something keeps telling me that if you really love Emily, which I think you do, you should let her into your secrets. She might be shocked at first, but with time, she will come over it and help to galvanize us into a formidable force to counter this evil. This evil that's is almost spreading like cancer. I know what you are thinking. You're thinking that once Emily knows the secrets, then her pastor will be involved, and then the whole church might know about it through his preaching. No this won't be so. We shall have a secrecy pact, an agreement, and a confidentiality bond that would make it difficult if not impossible for this matter to go public. Trust me KD. I will do it". Silas always has a way with words. He was not going to do anything, but loves to bamboozle his friend with big grammar.

There was a long pause from KD. He was thinking how this was going to be possible. He was thinking what kind of strategy Silas would use to accomplish this. What game

plan to achieve the goals of keeping this secret while battling the evil forces at the same time.

The stress on KD was already showing. KD got more confused. He could not imagine himself revealing everything to Emily. However he is comfortable to reveal just enough to put Emily in the picture of what is going on between him and the negative supernatural. After trying to make KD understand, Silas in his usual style, started using more confused language to knock KD into submission. He used the suicidal feelings and attempts by KD to impress on him that it was now or never. Silas had saved him from the first and second suicide attempts so, he told him that he was not doing it a third time. Silas told him, "My brother, you know that I am always there for you, and that whenever they rush you to the hospital for any emergencies, I am always the first person they call as your next of kin". KD interrupted. "OK, should I let her into the secrets when I must have taken off to Nigeria?" "No!" Replied Silas. "You should speak to her face to face before you go

anywhere." Silas was glad with this new development. He was beaming with smiles which KD couldn't see. He continued, "If you cannot see her face to face, then arrange a phone call and have a long conversation with her. Remember we have two lives at stake here. Two precious lives!" KD interrupted again, "Don't forget these evil forces are still monitoring me. They could appear on the scene if I decide to meet her face to face, and make matters even worse. Anyway, I shall arrange a phone call tomorrow". Silas did not want any further waste of time, so he cut in. "My bro, don't put forward till tomorrow what you can do today. That is what our elders used to say." "OK I will call her today". Replied KD. "Hopefully we can sort this out before weekend".

Silas felt a few inches taller, with the kind of joy that hits a man after signing a billion dollar contract. He knew there was no going back. He knew he had a very stubborn friend who will do whatever has been agreed. In fact, he is known to exceed expectations in some cases. Now, all he had

to do was to watch, pray and hope that Emily is carried along.

But how did KD plunge so low that all he now thinks about is committing suicide, or running away to a far country where nobody will find him? How did he start this journey with the occult world? How did it all begin?

Chapter Two

Connecting With Absalom

In life, it takes two to tango, and a third person to play the music. The trio in this story are the spirits of Ahithophel, Absalom and Satan the Devil.

The time this battle started raging was around 1050BCE when David was king of Israel.

Ahithophel was the most trusted counsellor of King David the anointed one, the man after God's heart. The King was so close to the Heart of God, that the Bible calls him a friend of God.

Absalom was the most handsome, intelligent, and most loved man amongst David's children. Just as God loved Satan, and Satan the Devil rebelled against Him,

wanting to be like the Most High, Absalom envied his father and Satan capitalized on it to do his damage.

Ahitophel and Absalom had something in common. They had something in their hearts against David, so it was easy for David's enemy number one to connect the two. Ahitophel had bitterness and Absalom had envy. Satan the enemy quickly connected the two, so that Ahitophel conspired with Absalom and betrayed King David.

Ahitophel finally ended his life tragically by committing suicide, while Absalom never lived long to smell the throne of his father.

Satan never wants to accept defeat so, he had to fashion two of his top ranking devils to carry on with the legacy of Ahitophel and Absalom. This was how Absalom was programmed to manipulate men whose hearts were envious towards their biological and spiritual fathers and elders.

In the church, Satan had capitalised on this envy between fathers and young pastors, to cause mayhem. This was how he trapped

Kaye Dubaye, alias Pastor KD, when he fell for this temptation.

The devil who loves to steal, to kill and to destroy, seizes every opportunity of such envy to empower lower demons and other agents to manipulate men and women and lure them into more sin.

It is worth remembering at this stage that these demons are spirits and do not die. They just get recycled for more deplorable assignments.

When the devil perceived that the young pastor KD had envy and lust buried in his heart, he moved quickly to capitalise on this grave mistake and got his demons put to work immediately.

It is easy to think that KD was being tempted to sin against his "spiritual fathers", but the truth is that KD was drawn away of his own lust, and was enticed. He even went a step further to seek supernatural powers through a cult, which he hoped would help launch him to greater heights, and stand the chance of displacing his spiritual and biological fathers.

KD was initially humble, serving in a local church in Zambia. The hunger for fame and money made him to do things he never imagined he could do years back, because there was a void created in his heart.

KD stumbled on a continental cult group, based in Ghana with branches all over Africa, including Nigeria and Zambia. They promised to satisfy the void in his heart by introducing him to a new religion in town. This religion promised to give him the fame and fortune he so much desired.

While in Zambia, KD as "Assistant Pastor" was going through depression. He decided to take a holiday from the ministry and travelled to Nigeria, to chill out with friends. He was always searching for something more, something that would fill the void in his life, and something that would make him more famous than all the big pastors in the land.

One day, while he was holidaying in Lagos Nigeria with his friends, he met a certain seer from Ghana who promised him spiritual powers to make him rich and famous. He had joined this public transport heading to Oshodi Lagos from Coconut Bus stop, when the man approached him. He purported to know so much about KD, and promised him spiritual power without human sacrifice. He also promised to bring him enlightenment and fulfilment. Desperate for a sense of purpose, he agreed without much hesitation, believing completely in this seer.

They planned the journey to Ghana by road, taking off from Mile 2 Lagos.

The journey lasted twelve hours taking them through the Republic of Benin, and then Lome in Togo, before they crossed into Ghana. There was so much security checks ranging from Customs and Excise, Immigration and Drug Law Enforcement Agency all over the place. This gave KD the confidence that this road network they are following must be safe and secure. He felt that it was unlikely that these people would kidnap him, in view of the weight of evidence that these guys were international.

On arrival in Accra Ghana, KD was checked into a three star hotel. This hotel was carefully chosen because of its proximity to the chief priest and other occult grandmaster wannabes. The hotel also provided good views from the hilltop and KD enjoyed the food as well.

The next day, the chief priest got in touch with KD in the hotel to arrange for assessment, initiation, and induction. They set off very early in the morning before daylight through Accra-Cape Coast Road, to the headquarters, venue of the initiation.

Understanding KD's background was essential to the High Priest when the young man arrived for initiation. He had to reveal all his personal data. In a few months, he will be 20 years. A High School drop-out but with his mind intact and a vacuum in his heart or virgin temple for Absalom to pack in and possibly live forever.

KD revealed that he was prepared to do anything for fame and money, and would self-develop himself so he could stand on the same platform as all the big men of God who had university degrees. He told the High Priest, "I believe with enough money I can buy a degree and be addressed as Doctor Kaye."

He also loved women in the choir and thought they were takeaways for the Pastors. When probed further by the High Priest, he confessed to him, "I hope to marry my High school girlfriend, but keep some concubines in the church. I think this is how it is done nowadays." The High Priest laughed and replied, "They say power without control is dangerous." He continued, "Those men of God you just described have power without control. Here, in our church, there are controls. We have a set of rules that prophets must strictly follow." He explained further, "After the initiation, you will be handed over a box of commandments and connected to angels that only you can see. They will make sure things go on according to our plans and purposes.

KD agreed with the Chief Priest and submitted himself for initiation. On the day of initiation it was laid bare to him that according to the rules of the occult, there must be a victor and the vanquished in this battle between father and son. If the father does not die, then the son has to die. The spirit of death, which must be invoked, must not return without the mission being accomplished. The Chief Priest asked him, "Are you ready to proceed without looking back?" He replied, "Yes sir. I can't wait to be as big as my father or even bigger." Having cornered KD up to this point, the Chief Priest was not in a hurry. He wanted to explain to KD all the implications, so he went further. "We are going to do two things. The first one will be to give you a very strong guardian angel. This angel will make sure that within a very short time, your father will die so you can take over. Before then we will have to marry you to a woman in the marine world who will give you all the powers you need to stand in the office of your father." He continued, "Because of your age and experience, these two deities will make sure that you are well nurtured and protected for the assignment ahead is great." He went into more details; frightening details to check if KD will be shaken to withdraw. "If your father is so strong that he does not die, then you, the son, will have to die in his place. This is because your guardian angel must finish the job and kill somebody. What does this mean? There is a spirit of death, another angel, sent by Satan, through godfather Absalom, to accompany your guardian angel. These spirits do not work alone; they must have a partner for a perfect mission to be accomplished."

While he was saying all this, the mind of this teenager, about to enjoy his twentieth birthday in a few weeks, was boggling. He had questions for the chief priest.

Now because he had promised his secondary school heartthrob that he would marry her, his questions were centred on the area of relationships. He fired the first shot. "What will happen to my fiancée whom I have promised to marry? We have been courting for the past 2 years." He replied KD, "A soldier of the Godfather does not concern himself with the affairs of this world." He continued, "Once you are in it, you will be married to a more superior being. You must now learn to forget your earthly girlfriends." KD was not satisfied with this response, so he asked further; "Sir, are you implying that I will never get married at all?" "No my son," he responded. "The task ahead of you is so great that marriage will be a distraction. Take a look at me I am not married and I have everything. I have all the money and fame I need, and of course many children. Haven't you heard from the scriptures, that those who do not have biological children have even more children than those who have biological children?"

KD had more questions. This time, about his "spiritual father", whom he hopes to depose one day, and inherit his vast properties, congregation and fame. He believes in his heart that once he gets his hands on his spiritual father, the senior pastor of their church, then getting his hands on the biological father will be a piece of cake. With this in mind, he went on to get a clearer picture from the chief priest.

KD went on to ask, "Supposing we do not get rid of my spiritual father, can I still succeed in getting rid of my biological father so I can inherit his earthly properties?" The chief priest had a long pause, looking for a better way to break the bad news to KD. He responded, "You see the Grand Master, Absalom works with other angels to make sure you succeed. However if you do not succeed in providing all the necessary sacrifices to eliminate your spiritual father, unfortunately, the angels, especially the one in charge of death, will have to strike at you instead. So you must make sure you provide all the necessary sacrifice to grease the wheel of progress, because the task ahead is huge, and the result if well managed, can make you the most famous in this land."

With KD a bit shaken by the revelations of the day, he thought there was no need for further questions. He then asked that the chief priest should take him to the place of rest so he could do his usual prayers. The accommodation provided for him was not very far. It was just a single bed apartment. The apartment was just enough for him to lay his head and rest, while getting ready for the sacrifice and initiation.

Now KD remembered that on the way coming to meet the chief priest, a lot of kids were loitering around, some playing games and entertaining themselves. He never knew that those were the kids who were used for sacrifices of this nature, for the initiation and for power upgrade. He only discovered this years later. They had told him from day one, that everything they would do, will not involve human sacrifice.

When KD reached his single bed apartment to rest, he perceived the smell of stale blood in the room. He wasn't sure where the smell was coming from. He just assumed that there must have been some slaughtering of chicken and goats behind the lodge.

KD tried to catch a nap and a short prayer before the midnight initiation.

In the one hour sleep, he had a dream.

He was being chased by dogs in the dream.

The chasing started from a forest with footpaths.

He ran and ran until he busted onto a beach, a sandy area.

This sand did not allow him to run as fast as he wanted.

And the dogs were still chasing.

Then all of a sudden a man appeared.

The man looked like his spiritual father.

KD could hardly speak but only pointed backwards to the dogs, to show the man why he was running.

Then the spiritual father bent down and hit the sand on the beach with his palms. He packed a handful of sharp sand from the beach and threw the sharp sand on the dogs that were chasing after the young man.

Then all of a sudden the dogs ran backwards barking, and continued running until they disappeared.

He woke up panting and was breathing heavily.

He didn't understand what the dream meant.

He knew he couldn't reveal this dream to the chief priest just yet, neither could he tell anyone at this point.

One thing he understood; he must have been powerless for dogs to chase him in the dream.

He felt like having a shower.

The room was now getting hot.

It looked like the fan was blowing hot air.

He picked up his towel and gently cleaned the sweat off his body.

Now he couldn't wait for the initiation to come and go.

At the initiation, KD was unconscious throughout the ceremony.

He did not know what happened in the proceedings. They probably drugged him, so he won't see what was used for the sacrifice.

His anger was that he did not experience any dreams or observe any unusual spiritual incidents during the unconscious moment. He only woke up with pains from incisions made probably with razor blades on his back and thighs.

The sharp pain made him believe that he was still alive.

But the presence of strange looking beings standing side by side with the chief priest, made him think otherwise. "Am I in heaven or hell?" was the overwhelming thought in his head. The response from the chief priest confirmed to him that someone must be reading his mind, and accurately too.

"Stand up son", was the swift response from the priest. "Let me introduce you to your new friends."

KD was now fully alert but tense. He responded with a shaky voice. "Who are these?"

Now, the spirit beings that will work with KD in his new ministry were there. The only missing companion was his beautiful marine wife called Kikki, and of course the big boss Absalom who hardly appears on such small occasions. Some faithful members call him Godfather, while some call him the Devil as he usually delegates assignment to lower angels or demons in his capacity as the supreme spirit of evil. As the Devil, he is always at enmity with God, and having the power to afflict humans both with bodily disease and with spiritual oppression that are physically tormenting.

The Chief Priest noticed the surprise on KD's face and decided it was time to explain things now that he is fully awake.

He explained all about the spirit beings hanging around. "In your case, young man, the reinforcing angel doubles as a guardian and a messenger spirit. As a messenger spirit, the angel operates by collecting information about people and passing it on to you for a reward". He continued, "This spirit becomes your source of wealth and influence. The only thing that keeps them loyal is regular sacrifice. With this angel, whatever you ask your flock will be given to you. If members of your church have to borrow or steal to bring you gifts, they will do so without hesitation, as long as you ask." He continued, "The secrets of your flock will be known and given to you free of charge. It is your duty to know how to use this information to extort money from them by prophesying all kinds of prophesies. The secrets of your flock will be stolen and given to you free of charge. That is the duty of these angels. It is your duty to now use this information to extort money from them by prophesying and making demands". He continued. "Not all demands can be met unless you upgrade. At the upgraded level, you will be given a specially blessed white chalk which you will rub on your tongue before speaking to your flock, to make things easy."

He changed the topic to focus on the marine wife, Kikki, who was absent at this meeting. He reiterated, "if you had married before this initiation ceremony, then your earthly wife's business and health will be hit with problems to frustrate both parties and set the ball rolling for a divorce, so that you can be free and devote more of your time to this assignment and to our godfather."

After the week of assessment, initiation, and induction they set off very early in the morning through Nsawam Road, Accra to meet up with some devotees at R5 Bus stop, opposite Princeway Hotel Avenor, so they could all travel together by road to Nigeria.

They all had their rucksacks packaged neatly by Chief Priest himself. In the rucksack was all the memorabilia including the magical box containing the Ten Commandments from Absalom the "Godfather".

Chapter Three

How He Got Oppressed

Initially, everything seemed fine after the initiation. The members of the cult were friendly and welcoming, and KD felt like he had finally found his place in the world.

He was given a wife from the marine world and she was over-possessive. There was no way he could connect with other women, and his relationship with his long standing girlfriend, Emily, was threatened.

On the business front, he was doing well initially with the help of the dwarf angels assigned to him. His popularity was rising slowly every day. He treated his church like a proper worldly business, constantly reminding his lieutenants about the need to always stay profitable. He was gifted. He inherited his business acumen from his biological father. There was no doubt that with the kind of support he received physically amongst his lieutenants, he could achieve great heights with the correct foundation and mentorship. But he relied heavily on his spiritual guidance from his occult masters and angels. He gave no proper chance to learning or self-development. Being a drop out from school, he believed he could cash in on the inborn and inherited business acumen and spiritual guidance from his guardian angels. But he was limited in capacity and scope. Like a car built with a specific engine capacity, he could not perform more than his capacity.

He was at the mercy of this secret cult and his guardian angels. They allowed him to make money to a certain level, beyond which he had to make bigger sacrifices. Of course nothing is free from Satan and no gift comes from his devils without sorrow. At one stage he had four cars parked in his garage. This included a flashy sports car and the 4x4 Jeep that was given to him as a gift from one of his church members. He believed he was doing well, in fact better than his age mates.

In his early twenties, he thought he had arrived. He thought he had made it big. But his target was to overtake the big pastors in Africa. He wanted to be bigger than men of God who were older, smarter and better educated than him. He reasoned with himself, that the best way to achieve this target, will be to submit to a popular well anointed man of God, and accept him as a spiritual father. In other words, he decided he would play double standards. He would submit to this popular man of God, learn more tricks of the business of church building and growth, and use the occult powers to move forward. He believed that no one will ever find out the source of his powers.

Choosing the man that KD will work under was not easy at all. This took him to travel widely in Africa, searching for "The man of God". He went between Nigeria, Ghana and South Africa. He had his criteria well laid out. One of the criteria was that his mentor or spiritual father must not dig deep into his past. The spiritual father must be someone who will accept him as he is. His spiritual father must not pass him through deliverance ministration. His spiritual father must not question his association with members of the opposite sex. His spiritual father must not investigate his source of wealth.

He resigned from his local church in Zambia to stay solo for a while. He wanted to spend 3 months finding his feet and aligning with a man of God that he could be proud to call his spiritual father.

He spent three months in three different churches in Nigeria, Ghana, and South Africa, before choosing where he would pitch his permanent tent.

He started getting more popular under his spiritual father, using this mentor to connect to foreign members. He was now open to international visitors, receiving gifts and cash in foreign currencies. With this progress he decided that time was ripe to open a church branch that will look like it was part of his mentor's church. He was now prepared to live and run his church like a parasite until the time was ripe to secede and do damages to his spiritual father.

UPGRADING HIS SPIRITUAL POWER

As time went on, things started to get strange. The cult started to ask for more sacrifices. If the sacrifices were chicken, bulls and goats, KD wouldn't mind. He begged them to accept goats but they wouldn't bulge. They wanted his mother or girlfriend Emily. This would be the most expensive sacrifice they have demanded of him.

How could they ask him to sacrifice his sweet mother or his best friend and future wife? The thought of this demand gave him regular headaches and anxiety. He tried several times to take up the issue with the Chief Priest to no avail.

The cult coordinator or Chief Priest, began to speak of dark forces and demon angels that were watching them at all times. He claimed that their only protection was to remain devoted to the cult and its beliefs.

KD tried to brush off the strange behaviour, but soon he began to experience strange things himself. He would wake up in the middle of the night to find his room very hot, even though the air-conditioner was on full blast. He would hear whispers and footsteps in the hallway, even though he was alone in the house. And worst of all, he began to feel an overwhelming sense of dread whenever he was near the chief priest and the other cult members, all camouflaging as seers or church prophets.

At first, KD tried to ignore his fears. He convinced himself that it was all in his head, that he was just being paranoid. But then, one night, something happened that he couldn't explain. He was sitting alone in his room when he felt a cold breath on the back of his neck. He turned around to see a shadowy figure standing in the corner of the room, staring at him with glowing red eyes. KD screamed and ran out of the room, his heart pounding with fear.

After that night, things only got worse. KD began to have nightmares about demons and evil spirits tormenting him. He started to see strange symbols carved into the walls of the cult's meeting place, symbols that made him think of ancient curses and black magic. And worst of all, he felt like he was being watched all the time, like something was following him wherever he went.

Eventually, KD realized that he had made a grave mistake by joining the cult. He knew that he needed to get out before it was too late. But it wasn't going to be easy. Chief Priest and the other members had become his whole world, his only friends and family. He didn't know how to leave without facing their wrath. It became even worse and unbearable when he couldn't sleep with his girlfriend. It was either the girlfriend was given a body odour that KD felt like throwing up thereafter, or her business was attacked with many losses over a range of products she was selling.

Few attacks also came through embarrassing situations in his "occultic church" anytime he fails to offer the right type of sacrifice. Sometimes his prophesies will go so wrong, he will wish the earth will just open up and swallow him.

Another embarrassing situation he is not in a hurry to forget, is the demand by one of his flocks for a refund of his seed offering. In that incident one of his highest donors or sponsors as they were called, had a prophecy regarding his business. In order to seal the prophecy, he was asked to sow a seed with his big SUV. He did sow the seed, and waited patiently for almost a year, but nothing happened. He couldn't wait any longer, so he started to demand the return of his SUV. It was a scandal that rocked his "occultic church" for a long time.

Another embarrassing moment in his church was when an agent of the marine world infiltrated his choir team. She eventually got to sleep with KD and put the show on the rumour mill and on social media.

Towards the end of the year, it was this close girlfriend, Emily who helped KD escape the occult. Together, they plotted a way to sneak out of the cult's compound in the dead of night, when he had gone to renegotiate his sacrifice. It wasn't until they were far away that KD felt like he could breathe again.

He knew he would never forget the terror he had experienced while he was a member of that cult, but he also knew that he had survived at least for a short time. And that was something to be grateful for. He who fights and runs away lives to fight another day.

Details of the escape and battles that followed, including suicide attempts, are dealt with in the next chapters and series.

Chapter Four

Opening Doors for the Devil

While in Ghana and later in Zambia, KD went through a tough period of orientation with the chief priest. During this period, the chief priest focused more energy in preparing the young man for future attacks, the ones from the positive, and the ones from the negative supernatural.

According to the Chief Priest, "Whether you are on God's side or the Devil's side, there will be attacks. Most of the attacks are to position you for promotion." But what about attacks on his loved ones like Emily? This was where the Chief Priest was silent.

KD was not told why and how these attacks would come. They were meant to keep him solitude and devoted to the course. Devoted only to his spiritual grandmaster or messengers, and bonded only to his very jealous marine wife. As one who aspires to be great in the occult kingdom, he had to contend with two masters - One financial god the other sexual god, both loyal and reporting to Absalom grandmaster devil, nicknamed "Godfather".

BONDING

Bonding to a sexual god was the first gift he received after initiation. Christians call them spiritual wives. Here in this kingdom, they are spiritual gods sent to satisfy all sexual desires, so KD will never be desperate to look elsewhere.

The night of introduction and bonding was so simple KD couldn't believe his eyes. All he had to do was to repeat a certain word seven times. Christians will probably think he was speaking in tongues. At the seventh time of repeating this word, the spiritual guardian or wife will appear.

He was alone in the room and enjoying his glass of wine when he decided to call out the magical words seven times. "Kuje biasulla kikki, kuje biasulla kikki, kuje biasulla kikki...." There and then appeared a very beautiful lady in his room. This was his spiritual guardian or marine wife.

Her skin was dark and lovely. She had eyes like a diamond, her cheeks were comely with rows of jewels and glittering earrings, her neck with chains of gold. He thought this might be the popular Queen of the coast. He said to himself, "This lady is really beautiful with the right curves in the right places." She wore a perfume that could breakdown any room odour in seconds.

She was gorgeously adorned with ornaments, with rings on her fingers and ears. KD had never seen such a beauty before. She got closer to KD with open arms to hug him. He developed cold feet and stepped back a bit not sure what to do. "Relax my darling" she said, "It's me your wife your sex slave, your guardian. You called me. You are now my master and I am your slave. Do to me whatever you like."

Immediately she fell on her knees and asked KD to put on the robe he got from chief priest, and then come and lay his hands on her head. "We must put certain things in practice today. Please do not put on any pair of trousers or boxer shorts." She demanded. "No problems" KD responded.

KD could not believe his ears. His mouth was slightly opened in amazement, upon hearing this beautiful lady speak. He tried to contain himself and wondered, "If truly she is my slave, then she must do all I ask her to do. Now I can satisfy all my sexual fantasies".

KD got a bit bold and asked her, "By the way, what is your name?" "Kikki" she replied. "I am yours forever. You don't need to look for a woman again for the rest of your life. I am all yours. But one thing you must understand, I am very jealous. I cannot share you with another woman."

KD returned to his senses when he discovered that this was not an illusion. He sipped his drink, and then opened his arms, hugged her, and went to change into his pastoral office regalia. Not long, he started a long romance that ended with sex.

KD never had this kind of sex before. "This is better than good and sweeter than sweet," he told her. He knew straightaway that he was not dealing with an ordinary human being. During the sexual romp, he started wondering in his heart if he could try out his sexual fantasies. To his shock, the lady knew his thoughts. She paused wriggling her waist for a moment, looked him in the eyes, and said, "Those fantasies in your heart, you can now enjoy because I am very flexible. Don't worry". KD knew after this, that his appetite for other women would be tested in the very near future.

One thing that surprised KD was the fact that he was never exhausted during or after the romp. With his girlfriend, Emily, after the first round he got tired and could not go on till the next day. "So what is Kikki doing to make me go this extra mile without getting tired?" He asked himself. "Is it because she did most of the physical work? Is it because she probably put something in my drink? Is it because her strong perfume was energizing?" He was still deep in his thoughts when Kikki stood up, dressed up and got ready to kiss him goodbye. KD wanted some more, but she was eager to go until next time. This was because daylight was fast approaching. She must be 'home' before sunrise. According to their custom, sunrise meeting her outside will spell doom for both parties.

While she was putting finishing touches to her makeup, pretending she was all human, the young man wanted to chat a little so he could ask some questions. "Not this time", she told him. "Maybe when I come again".

They kissed goodbye and KD opened the door for her to step out into the unknown. "She didn't even need the door", KD thought, staring at her backside as she disappeared. This was a sight he was not going to forget in a hurry. Her skin-tight white trousers had a matching green top, with white embroidery around the breasts, reminded him of the Nigerian flag of green–white-green. Luxurious hair, well braided, with high heel shoes that can only befit a queen. KD gazed at her until she disappeared. He said to himself, "If this is not the queen of the coast, I wonder where the queen of the coast is? Who is Kikki?"

He went straight to bed, and imagined how he will cope in the coming weekends when Emily would pay her usual weekend visits. Will Kikki visit him also? How will he shield Emily from Kikki?

Absalom the grandmaster had programmed one of the attacks on his sexual partners including Emily. The atmosphere for attacks on Emily and all his sexual partners was easy to create, now that Kikki had planted invisible demons to monitor KD. In the physical world they are known as monitoring and bugging devices.

To make things easy for KD or his woman to get attacked, all he had to do was to lust after any woman.

For KD there was no question of falling in love. There is no such thing in this kingdom. Having a steady girlfriend was forbidden. Having a wife was inconceivable. That Emily has been steady for months, beats his imaginations. But she had a fair share of the attacks.

The first weekend after the visit of Kikki approached, and KD was really apprehensive, knowing what could happen. Emily did not know about Kikki, but has been looking forward to this weekend to be with her man. She visits him every other weekend after work.

At the office, Emily glanced at the clock, sighing in relief as she saw the hands strike five. It had been a long and arduous day at work, and she couldn't wait to finally be home in the arms of her boyfriend, KD. As she gathered her belongings, she felt a slight tremor of anticipation course through her. She knew KD would be waiting for her, eager for their intimate union after a week of longing for one another.

With her heart pounding in her chest, Emily made her way through the city streets, her mind filled with thoughts of the passionate evening that awaited her. She loved how KD, nearly twenty one years old, was older than her by a few months. His maturity and confidence were incredibly attractive, making her crave his touch even more.

As Emily approached their apartment, she took a deep breath to calm her racing pulse. The scent of home enveloped her as she turned the key in the door, stepping into the familiar space they shared every other weekend.

She wanted to relax first. She wished she had a massage parlor in KD's home and that her man would give her a good massage during this visit. This was wishful thinking. She went straight to the bathroom to wash herself thoroughly. She went in with things to scrub her feet and remove those rough edges off the sole of her feet. It was a long bath. She took her time and while putting finishing touches, she heard the door unlock, and in her mind, she thought, "that must be my man. I wish he could come in here and give me a good massage."

Emily hurried out of the bathroom when she discovered that KD was not forthcoming. She found him lying on the bed in boxer shots. "Hi darling, I knew that was you so I quickly finished what I was doing to be with my king." KD was just gazing at Emily without saying a word. He was wondering in his heart how lucky he was to be in a relationship with this beauty. Emily had only her large white towel wrapped round her curvaceous body.

Not long they were kissing, and one thing led to another. Then something happened. A strong pungent smell hit KD badly. It smelt like one of those rotten unhatched eggs from his mother's poultry way back in the village. The stench was coming from in-between her legs and only KD could perceive it. Then he realized he was under severe attack from the marine world. His own marine wife was at it again. Under sixty seconds, Emily realised that his manhood has come down and shrunk considerably. There was no need to proceed any further.

He had gone through this before with other women. He knew that he was the only one who perceived it. He felt helpless and in fear.

Emily was highly disappointed. She was confused. She did not know what had happened, and why her man all of a sudden had his manhood shrink, to spoil their love making. She deserves an explanation. "What is going on darling?" She asked. "It's like I have just been shot by a missile loaded with a pungent gas." He replied. "Did you perceive anything?" Emily's response was a simple "No!"

Emily was still in shock. She thought her boyfriend was playing a game. Her suspicion that other girls have been playing games with KD is now almost confirmed.

KD did not panic. It had happened with other girls and he knew the source of the attack. He knew that it was the jealous marine wife given to him during his initiation. He knew that there was absolutely nothing he could do about it.

This was the embarrassing incident that pushed Emily closer to God. Over the weeks she prayed and fasted. She later went to see her pastor for counselling.

The pastor she met for counselling was a famous pastor in South Africa. During the counselling she was advised to surrender her life to Jesus Christ and together they will fight to win back her man. She was advised that the process may be long but will surely not fail. She was advised to avoid premarital sex and to keep her body holy because her body is the temple of the Holy Spirit. The Pastor assured her that God wanted to use her big time, if she can avoid falling into temptation and try to stay committed to her God.

She visited the pastor in South Africa, for many days of prayers and deliverance. During one of such visits, the pastor revealed that KD had renounced Jesus Christ and accepted another God.

On many visits, the pastor had a fair share of temptation. Each time he wondered who on earth will stand the sight of this beautiful lady, and not be tempted. She was young, intelligent, pretty and well-endowed with very curvaceous body. The pastor found himself fighting temptation all the time, and he kept winning all the time.

EMILY AT THE CROSSROAD

Meanwhile, Emily was at a crossroad. She was about to lose KD. Will she completely lose KD now that she has abstained from sex? Will the other girlfriends capture him and win the trophy? By this time she did not know that her major competitor was from the marine world and a senior marine spirit for that matter. A senior devil that could possibly take the life of her man, and they will never see him again.

She thought deeply about it, whether to go into this battle physically and compete with other girls for her man, or whether to go into it spirituality through prayers.

Emily spend most of her prayer time meditating on what could possibly make the young man like KD renounce Jesus Christ, drift way from God and drift towards Satan like this. She spent time studying the Bible. She remembered that her man was spiritual and a church pastor. She remembered her man's favourite Bible chapter in Psalm 23. She spent time studying this Psalm to hear what God is saying through the scripture. From this one chapter, she came across a lot of revelations which changed her prayer life.

What were these revelations that changed her prayer life?

Chapter Five

Atmosphere for Demonic Attacks

Kaye Dubaye or KD as he was known among his friends, lived a life that attracted demons ever before he joined the occult church. But that was on a small-scale.

His large-scale communion with evil spirits started during his initiations into the occult church which he had not revealed to Emily. His first big mistake was to renounce Jesus Christ on his day of initiation. He was seduced to another god. He was deceived into believing that his new found religion had higher powers and could bring him instant success, and make him famous.

What he did not understand was that he would lose all the benefits of being a child of God. His favourite Psalm 23 could no longer apply. This is most people's favourite Psalm that itemizes the benefits of a child of God.

Because he renounced Jesus Christ, it meant the Lord will no longer be his shepherd. As the Lord was no longer his shepherd, three major changes happened; he now was perpetually in want all his days. The Lord will not make him lie down on green pastures or lead him beside still waters. He could not restore his soul anymore or guide him in the paths of righteousness. This lack of benefits created open doors for the devils to walk freely into his life and control him.

Other fallout from this renouncement of Jesus Christ was that KD turned himself into an enemy of the Kingdom of God. He had pitched himself against the most potent force in the universe.

Also by renouncing the Lordship of Jesus Christ, he started to attract all the opposites of the benefits that is reserved for children of God. He became more insatiable and always in want. Money was never enough, a woman was never enough, and wine was never enough. His wanton appetite took him higher to cocaine addiction. He was now at the mercy of the devils. He could now be easily and remotely controlled. At one stage, as a visiting prophet to a local church in Zimbabwe, he couldn't mount the stage unless he was high on cocaine. Occasional brandy and whisky became a habit.

What about the area where Jesus Christ restores the soul? Whereas Jesus enlivens our soul, quickens our mortal body, it was the reverse for KD. In his case, the devil bought his soul and messed it up. There was no life in it. He could not connect to the Almighty God anymore. In fact, he was a walking corps; dead body walking. Even his "Godfather" couldn't connect.

His soul was so messed up, he was then inhabited by the spirit of suicide, the demon that was sent to finish the job and pull KD into hell and eternal fire. Thank God for the mercies of our Lord Jesus Christ who saves and delivers those who call on His name.

According to that popular Psalm 23, children of God will walk through the valley of the shadow of death, and will fear no evil because God is with them. KD on the other hand was always scared to be alone in his room, and will often scout around for loose women to spend the night with. This he did regularly, but was interrupted from time to time by the presence of his marine wife. He did not know that he was creating the perfect atmosphere for demonic torments and oppression.

The fear factor was huge. There was no time the marine wife appeared that did not get KD frightened. The wife had to announce all the time, "It's me, my darling, don't panic."

The fact that he renounced Jesus Christ meant that perfect love was now absent from his life. The word of God tells us that there is no fear in love, and that perfect love casts out fear. Jesus Christ who is the perfect love, had nothing to do with KD after the renunciation.

When KD renounced Jesus Christ, he didn't know he was renouncing goodness and mercy. Even though he was enjoying some form of wealth from the devils, he was struggling everyday with big problems which he believed his occult church would solve. Each time they will ask for a bigger sacrifice to solve a problem. By the time they asked for a human sacrifice, he knew there was no going forward with the cult. At the beginning when he joined, they had promised him there will never be any human sacrifice. Now they are not just asking for any human sacrifice. They are asking for his sweetheart or his mother as sacrifice.

His problems were compounding every day, and he was under oppression from the evil forces; seven different forces altogether! He was dealing with rebellion from close lieutenants in his Church. His sweetheart Emily, was threatening to leave him permanently, since he could not sleep with her or marry her. His biggest sponsor in Church wanted his car back, and was threatening to involve the police. He was using fake immigration papers and the Immigration officers were trying to blackmail him. One of his friends was into drugs and has been locked up and KD was being asked to bail him out. To make matters worse, his mother was seriously ill. Also, the tax people were after him because he has been dodging taxes.

Sometimes when he is not thinking about committing suicide, KD just wants to relax and remember the good times he has enjoyed as the general overseer of his occult church. The memories of the good times had kept him going.

Chapter Six

Remembering the Good Times

The good times had started almost on KD's arrival at the airport, on his return from Ghana through Nigeria, after all the initiation ceremonies and "anointing" from the cult's divisional leader known as the chief priest.

He was given few memorabilia from the ceremonies, which also carried negative powers to entice, to captive, to hypnotise and even to enslave members of his congregation. One of them was made with the twisted horn of a ram, used as an improvised cellular device to communicate with the chief priest and the godfather. Another item made from the horn of a cow was used for commanding money from local sources, in local currency using his dwarf spirits as agents.

All these items were well packaged in his suitcase with old newspapers and cello tape. Customs officials could not detect them. In fact, none of his items was searched throughout his journey. The spirit and power he carried made it impossible for anyone to stop him and to search him.

When he arrived at the airport, back from the initiation ceremonies, members of his welcome entourage were there waiting. He had told them he was going to the mountain on a spiritual pilgrimage and would come back with higher powers to perform miracles signs and wonders.

On arrival, they felt the power straight away at the airport. He laid his hands on one or two of them to bless them and they staggered and nearly fell. Passers-by thought they were pretending to fall under the "anointing". The good times started from the airport. The entourage, his followers were busy fighting over who would carry his luggage. They believed his luggage also was anointed to bless. Mind you, at this stage, he had not pulled out of the church in Zambia to establish his own and move to South Africa. This was the beginning. This was the mother of all moves.

While they were busy planning how to entertain themselves when they get to the home of their assistant pastor, the young man was busy thinking and scheming how to pull out of Zambia and relocate to South Africa. He had already planned in advance by contacting an immigration agent to organise his papers for relocation to South Africa. This he did before travelling for the initiation ceremony.

Relocating to South Africa was going to be difficult, the agent had told him, but he was determined. He had to be in South Africa to blend in with genuine Bible believing churches. Many other objectives included bringing his camp closer to the church where his sweetheart worshipped and of course increasing his congregation with the impact of his occult powers.

If there was anything that bordered pastor KD, it was getting into South Africa. He did not have the required documents, but he believed that the black market immigration service should sort him out.

When the entourage arrived at his house, they were busy getting things to eat and drink. Their favourite handsome assistant pastor had just arrived after weeks of "fasting and prayers". To them, this was the time for feasting. As usual after fasting comes feasting. Already, the shopping and cooking had been contracted in advance to one of the choir members in advance by the organising committee. Nothing should go wrong with this merriment.

Pastor KD had other ideas. He was more interested in connecting with the immigration officer who was an immigration insider but had an agency that ran black market. His friend Silas connected this officer, so most times it was Silas who would take KD to his hideout. Fortunately, this time around, KD was able to connect directly so there was no need for Silas. KD invited the immigration officer to join them in his house. This way, they can mix business with pleasure. They can talk business over dinner and find KD's South Africa visa by hook or crook.

The welcome party started on time and the primary concern of the young man was how to obtain the visa and permanent stay in South Africa, and to end up the night sleeping with one of the choir girls. These two desires he achieved.

The immigration officer was around and well entertained. He promised to deliver at all cost. In his mind, he was planning to deliver fake documents from the black market. He planned to do it in such a way that KD will always be at his mercy. He planned to extort as much money from pastor KD when he crosses into South Africa.

Meanwhile the choir girls had come for the occasion in full force. KD was part of the choir before he was ordained assistant pastor. His favourite bed mate was around enjoying herself and hoping to sleep over when others have gone home. What she didn't realise was that she was going to be the first person to provide body fluids for KD's occult sacrifice. The chief priest had demanded that whenever he had sexual intercourse with a woman, he must provide a white handkerchief used to wipe the private part of the victim and scoop the vaginal fluid for sacrifice. This is a mandatory sacrifice which must be performed on a regular basis at any nearby beach or river. This sacrifice must be done in order to maintain his level of power.

This was the first of many nights of good times for Pastor KD. He will always use one stone to kill two birds.

Whatever he did here as assistant Pastor was small and a preparation for bigger things in South Africa. When he relocated, there was bigger congregation, more revelling, more sacrifices using female emissions in white handkerchiefs.

But to part ways with the local church and breakaway without problems or spiritual infighting, KD had to organise a night vigil planned for inner circle members who were very close to him. This way, false prophesies will be released. Organised prophesies to confirm what they already planned. They agreed that these prophesies will be detailed, confirming the name of the Church that will be founded by Pastor KD. The mandate of the church and mission statement will also be mentioned. Everything was planned. It will be made clear from these prophesies, that this new church will not be a branch of the main Zambian Church but autonomous in everything.

For this night vigil, KD decided to kill two birds with one stone. KD invited Silas, so he could be part of the move as a friend, and also relocate with him to South Africa. KD was in no mood to do away with this friendship with Silas, because relocating together will bring them closer to Emily, his South African born sweetheart.

The vigil kicked off at 11pm and lasted for three hours. KD needed some two hours in the morning to lay with a new girl, whose vaginal fluid must be used for sacrifice at the riverside early in the morning.

Silas was impressed with the entire proceedings and excited that KD was getting a lot more matured and prophetic at his age. He had a brief chat after the vigil. KD was a bit in a hurry because he needed time with the new girl. "Pastor KD, the young Daddy G.O," quipped Silas. "Very soon everyone is going to be calling you Daddy G.O." "Behave yourself Silas. This job is bigger than answering big names. I am really excited about moving to South Africa to start something new and to grow my congregation" Replied KD. "I am pleased with your support so far Silas. Have a good rest and I will probably see you tomorrow. I have an urgent business to attend to before daybreak." Silas wondered what kind of business could keep his friend up at this time.

Pastor KD went ahead with his business as planned. Fortunately, he was not bothered or disturbed by his marine wife. He got revitalised and more eager to relocate to South Africa.

Chapter Seven

Life after Relocation

Pastor KD kept in touch with his close friend Silas, not knowing that this would be part of his saving grace. He did not allow the relationship to grow very deep, so Silas did not know his cult secrets. KD thought he was playing safe so Silas will not reveal his secrets to Emily his girlfriend, or to his parents.

In relocating, KD had two objectives. Number one was to be rich and more famous than his spiritual fathers. The second objective was to mingle with the mainstream Bible believing churches in South Africa, and be seen as one of the genuine prophets in town.

To be rich and famous, he had to build and grow his congregation from hundreds to thousands in South Africa. This will involve a lot of sacrifices, both spiritual and physical. This will involve a lot of illicit, no-strings-attached sex, and many trips to the beach side for prayers. Consequently his new church must not be too far from the beach, where he would have to offer handkerchief sacrifices.

When the immigration papers were ready, he was invited to a meeting at a three star hotel in Zambia. At the meeting, he was introduced to two more "immigration officers." Some South African papers were handed over to him as the "permanent stay papers" that he would use to settle in South Africa and do his business. The only thing he must do is to travel by road with one of the officers present in that meeting. This officer was introduced as Felix, purporting to be a top ranking officer that will scale all the barriers and immigration checks with KD who did not realise his documents were fake.

When the discussion shifted to payments and settlement of the paramilitary forces at the borders, Felix at the meeting told KD. "You won't have to worry about settling all the police and immigration officers on the way. I will do all that." KD replied, "Fair enough, but how do I pay you back?" Felix responded, "It is all in the bill. You will only pay cash for my transportation, and as a man of God, you will bless us with any amount at the end of the journey when everything has worked well. The journey will take us through Zimbabwe, so we will be meeting at that central motor park next Friday morning before five."

The meeting ended with everyone happy and in high spirits. KD couldn't wait to check out of Zambia and relocate for good.

BETTER LIFE IN SOUTH AFRICA

The journey went ahead as planned and KD was so happy to finally fulfill his life time dream of living in South Africa. Even when he dropped out of school, he made an unsuccessful attempt to enter illegally. His experience as a very young teenager dropping out of school and running away from home to mingle with all the bad gangs, is enough to fill up a voluminous book. Now he thinks he is entering legally with a good chance of reconnecting with his sweetheart Emily, who coincidentally is now working in South Africa, and attends a Bible-believing Prophetic and Apostolic Church in Johannesburg.

One of the first persons that KD connected with by phone as soon as he arrived South Africa was his very good friend Silas. After a brief chat, KD told him, "Please remember to send me the details of Emily, especially where she works, so I can pay her a surprise visit one of these days, before I get too busy." The response from Silas was, "that is not a problem. I shall get that to you within a week. In fact, I plan to attend their church next Sunday in Johannesburg."

KD could not waste time to go into business. This is what he has been waiting for all these years. First, he wanted to check out of the hotel so he can get one closer to the beach. He reckons he might have to visit the beach every other day for the usual sacrifices to maintain his powers. This is the best he could do within his limited resources, instead of travelling all the way to Ghana for the big one.

He booked a three star hotel nearer the beach, and was comfortable with it. Being comfortable, he had to transfer his hidden luggage and items, including the chest or box containing the two stone tablets inscribed with their occult 10 commandments, and memorabilia from the boot of his car where they were being hidden from public view, to the hotel room. The night he got comfortable with a good room, he thought he could do with a new girl from a nearby college where the affluent usually arranged for party girls. He contacted his close friends excluding Silas so they could have an orgy. His plan was that after the orgy, he would select the one meant for vaginal fluid sacrifice. Unfortunately for him, this was the night his marine wife appeared unannounced. They were monitoring him from the Kingdom of darkness and knew when exactly to pop in. She had to come in and feel welcomed only when the horns and other objects of worship were inside the hotel and not in the car.

KD quickly cancelled his arrangement with the party girls when he got wind of the impending visit of the marine wife. While he was alone in the room, contemplating how to spend the rest of the night, his marine wife appeared. When she did appear, KD was shocked. "I wasn't expecting you." He muttered. "You should have told me you were coming."

Right in front of him was a beauty to behold, the marine wife looking very radiant, literally coruscating. This was his spiritual guardian especially at night.

Her skin was dark and lovely. She had eyes like a diamond, her cheeks are comely with glittering earrings dangling, her neck with chains of gold. He knew beyond any reasonable doubt that this was his marine wife. He said to himself, "This lady is really beautiful with the right curves in the right places, resembling Emily my sweetheart." She wore a perfume that could linger on for weeks. She was gorgeously adorned with ornaments, with rings on her fingers and toes. She got closer to KD ready for a hug and a kiss. KD did not wish to waste time at all. He went straight into the business of the day to hurriedly devour her, but wondered where his energy came from.

He noticed that before he went for the second round, she asked him to open his mouth. When he did, she dropped some tasteless ointment into his buccal cavity. "Why did you do that?" he asked. "This is to maintain your level of alertness and power till I return. Without this, you will be too exhausted to perform your official duties for a week or two."

He was happy to postpone his day of sacrifice for another day. He said to himself in the toilet, after the marine wife had gone. "Tomorrow is another day."

GROWING THE CONGREGATION

KD was now settled in South Africa, but did not know or expect he could be blackmailed by the same people who helped him cross over the border. He was living like "son of the soil", an indigene, a full citizen, and enjoying his occult Church. On Sundays he will perform "miracles" mixed with magic. During the week he will connect with his friends to go walking on alcohol and enjoying revelry and drunkenness, swimming in lewdness and lust, and flying on drugs. His part time hobby was to envy established men of God, especially those with Masters or Doctorate degrees.

By the time his congregation had grown from 100 to 1000 over a few years, he thought he had arrived. He looked himself in the mirror and said, "Now is the time to mingle with the big boys. Now is the time to pretend to run a genuine business, a bible believing Church. I must create more time to read the bible, so people will not perceive that I am not a genuine prophet, when I do not quote enough scriptures."

He was using the services of the dwarf angels to full benefit in collecting vital information about members of his congregation. He could get bank account details, phone numbers and perform magical signs. He was riding high and making money, serious money, including drug money. As long as he did not marry Emily, he felt he could do anything under the sun, according to the 10 commandments of the occult church.

He tried to keep in touch with Emily through his bosom friend, Silas. Emily was now born again and would not accept or honour any invitations. Her pastor was one of the popular ones in South Africa, so she wouldn't want anything to mar her image at the Church. She was very conscious of her image. In all these, his love for Emily never died.

SEEKING HIGHER POWER AND FAME

After about three years in the church business, he thought it was time to grow in power, in influence and in fame. He thought it was time to communicate directly with Absalom godfather. He spoke at length with chief priest on this matter. He kept waiting for quick response, but it never came. He went through some other members of the occult church, but nothing concrete happened. Then, after a few months of waiting, there came a reply from chief priest. It was not palatable. It was shocking. They were asking for bigger sacrifices before he could be hooked up to meet Absalom Godfather direct. They were asking for Emily or his mother as sacrifice. They wanted her blood and her private parts.

KD had not been feeling well since this bad news. The news was so bad, they even gave him a time limit. This news had changed the whole scenario. Will KD perform and lure Emily for sacrifice? Will he decline and be killed instead?

As the deadline was drawing nearer for him to submit Emily for sacrifice, the Kingdom of darkness was planting even more evil spirits to cage him. Topmost was the spirit of no marriage that accompanies the marine wife on assignment. By this time there were lots of scandals flying around concerning him and his occult church. The last straw that broke the camel's back was his adventure to betray some of the top Pastors in the country as a way of getting himself noticed and exposed to limelight. At this stage depression started setting in, and was fully blown within one year, leading KD to many failed suicide attempts.

Chapter Eight

Looking for Emily

KD's friend, Silas, was his next of kin. Any time there was a failed suicide attempt, Silas was the one they invited to the hospital to observe and stand by him.

On the third suicide attempt, Silas got so worried and fed up. He believed this was the best time to reconnect Emily and KD. He had the confidence that Emily could offer some support and possibly get her Pastors involved. "This one is above my skills." He always says to himself. He reminded himself of the background to this relationship, which he followed right from the start. Before they separated, Emily and KD had been dating for almost two years. They were both college students together and had a great relationship, until KD dropped out of school.

Emily was a young lady who had everything going for her - beauty, brains, and a loving family. She was in a happy relationship with her boyfriend, KD, who was a handsome and kind-hearted man with a great sense of humour. That was before he joined the league of cult members. Cult membership changed everything.

KD was a kind and caring boyfriend, always putting Emily first. He was also very spiritual and believed in the power of positive energy and good vibes, always yearning for more.

He got most of his traits and talents from his mother who was believed to be a prophetess. She was part of a Christian sect that went from house to house praying for people and getting blessed in return with material things.

Emily had always respected KD's beliefs, but had her reservations, knowing KD as Mummy's boy since school days. She hoped to meet his mother one day, believing they might get married in the future. However, that was about to change, after Emily heard rumours that KD was a member of a secret occult Church movement in Africa.

Coupled with bizarre things that happened during their intimate relationship in Zambia and now South Africa, Emily could not believe anymore. She just kept praying that God's will be done concerning their relationship.

As time went on, KD started having nightmares and these nightmares became more frequent and intense. He started experiencing physical symptoms like headaches and fatigue.

Emily heard about all these things happening to KD through Silas, and knew that something was very wrong, so she started doing her own research with her local pastor to find out what could possibly be going wrong with KD.

She discovered that there was a group of witches in their town who were known for their dark magic and their ability to harm others. She also discovered that there were wizards connected with a certain occult organisations in South Africa who take delight in tormenting weak Christians who profess Jesus Christ but are not prayerful enough to stand their ground.

Emily was shocked and frightened by what she had discovered, but she knew that she had to do something to help KD.

Meanwhile, Emily had been receiving Silas in her church to keep abreast of the mental health situation of KD. But she blamed Silas for aiding and abetting KD's occult journey from Zambia to South Africa. She believed that Silas knew so much about KD, which he always denied.

Emily spent quite some time explaining to Silas what she discovered about the dark forces, and how they use witches and wizards to oppress innocent people. She was proud to show off all the results of her research. She tried to prove that the people they attack most are the innocent ones and the weak Christians.

Silas had a different opinion. He believed that whatever KD was doing must have had side effects and that these side effects must have now kicked in. He believed that these side effects must have led to the many suicide attempts they witnessed in the past one year.

Silas agreed with Emily that as soon as KD got back to his feet, they will arrange a meeting so Emily can intercede with her pastor in this serious matter, because people believed this pastor was anointed for difficult matters.

Chapter Nine

The Discovery

One day, KD collected the home and church address from Silas and visited Emily, seeking for solutions to his problems. He was looking scared and confused. He told her that he had been experiencing strange things that he couldn't explain. He said he felt like he was being followed and watched and that he was having nightmares about witches.

Emily received him and tried to reassure him that it was just his imagination, but she could tell that he was genuinely frightened. She didn't know what to do, but she promised to support him no matter what. He was assured that everything will be kept confidential until the problem is solved. "You have nothing to worry about. Just tell me the whole story, my man". It has taken

KD this long to come this far in a chat about his occult church problems.

He had tried to avoid this conversation for a long time. But unfortunately, he promised himself and Silas, his best friend, that he has to reveal everything and find a permanent solution.

THE REVELATION.

KD first started to beat about the bush, explaining why he took his spirituality to a different level. He spoke on how much he loved his sweetheart, Emily, but the woman of his dreams was having a soft spot for prophets. He too wanted to be a prophet that is known nationwide and in most parts of Africa. But he just tried to explain his motivation, while Emily listened attentively.

Emily did not want to interrupt. Now that her man has decided to open up.
Now is not the time to interrupt. "I must allow the gist to flow." She spoke in her heart.

KD resumed the conversation. "You know after dropping out of school, I needed to do something with my life. I saw that one of the fastest growing businesses was the church business. They were organised and prospering. The prophets were respected and loved by women". Emily chipped in, "Are you speaking generally or you are referring to specific prophets?" KD replied, "I am speaking generally". He continued "The men of God were so organised, and they had a common purpose, to make as much money as possible. I spoke to a few of them. I got a few ideas. I heard the most educated of them all speak. I heard the least educated of them all. And in all, I saw that they were determined to succeed. I saw that they were determined to make as much money as possible off their flock. I knew from time that God commanded these shepherds to feed the flock. But then these men and women knew what they were doing. So I got in touch with one of them for mentorship. From there I was connected to young aspiring prophets. They were mentees under his care. I stumbled into one strange prophet from Ghana who showed me another way to make it faster. That way was probably not the best way from what I have now seen. I was with them and we travelled together. We went to different parts of Africa especially Ghana, where I was initiated. We got connected with an occult grandmaster. Things were moving smoothly. I thought I had found my career finally. They performed several sacrifices to help me. The sacrifices were not much. According to them all I needed was to bring some money. I was invited for super-initiation and induction. They made different initiations - three different types of initiations into the spirit world with messenger spirits called angels. The second type had to do with marine spirits or spiritual wife. Confident and comfortable, I waited for the big one, to meet with the 'Godfather'. I lacked nothing in those days. That was the time I was separated from you because they did not want me to see you again. After some time the relationship started turning sour. I knew this wasn't where I wanted to be. Here the devil was masquerading as angel of light. I thought this was where the real God was. I was made to denounce Jesus Christ. But I was wrong. I was wrong. I was definitely wrong."

KD got a bit emotional, took out his handkerchief to clean his nostrils, and then continued. "I started plotting my escape when they started asking for more sacrifices. They demanded sacrifices for the terrestrial spirits, sacrifices for the marine spirits including the spiritual wife. Then there is the big sacrifice to enable me meet with the 'Godfather', known as the Occult Grandmaster. The last sacrifice would have opened the door to limitless money. Their demand was for a human that I love very much."

Emily chipped in, "were they thinking of your mother?" "No!" Replied KD. "They were all in agreement that my fiancée will be the one." He looked Emily in the eyes and reassured her, "I can never sacrifice you for anything. See, to keep them happy, I made a promise".

Emily was now feeling uncomfortable. She initially thought she could handle this alone. Now this is looking bigger than she thought. In her mind, she was wondering. "Should I contact my pastor in the church? Should I go this alone?"

After a long pause, KD continue. "I have a plan. I think we should play along and pretend along. I know they are monitoring me, so let us pretend to dance to their tune, until I visit and collect my personal items from my cubicle at the camp in their South Africa branch. I believe they are using my personal items which have been bugged to trace me. In my escape master plan, we will visit my cubicle to assure them that I will keep to my promise. Then at midnight, we shall disappear with my personal items and jump the fence. We will need a lot of prayers to make sure nothing goes wrong."

Emily seemed to flow with this plan, but asked, "Should I contact the police so we have adequate cover outside the fence?" Kaye was quick to respond. "No, I'll be dead the next day. These guys enter secure rooms without passing through doors. You can only match them with spiritual powers. If you run with the Police to the sea, they have marine spirits there. If you run on land, they have terrestrial spirits. At night they have witches and wizards. You just have to consult a strong man of God before we take any risks."

After a long silence, Emily thought she knew how to approach the whole matter. She said she will make two phone calls immediately as this was urgent, and a matter of life and death. She pulled out her mobile phone and made appointments to see her church pastor the next day at the church office.

KD reminded her that time was not on their side. They had only one week to execute their plans before the Occult Grandmaster starts to look for him.

Emily seemed calm. She believed that once she got hold of her pastor, everything will be sorted. She holds her pastor in high esteem and believes anything is possible with God, through his hands. She tried for five minutes to promote the man of God, so that KD will feel confident to go with her.

Meeting her pastor the next day was very smooth and timely. The counselling went very well and they all agreed on a set of plans and a road map.

Chapter Ten

The Spiritual Battle

Emily knew that she had to join hands with her pastor to fight back against the witches and wizards who were attacking KD. She knew she needed some higher positive powers to deal with these negative elements.

She started studying spiritual practices and regularly attended deliverance ministration classes in her church. She also started using anointed oil to ward off negative energy and destroy negative influences.

She shared everything she had learned from her pastor with KD, and they started working together to protect him from the witches and wizards and occult powers. They also sought regular help of Emily's spiritual father, the General Overseer of the

Church who was able to provide them with additional protection and guidance.

Sometimes things get worse before they get better. KD's case got worse in the first few days of prayers. He nearly lost hope but Emily persisted.

Emily's world nearly came crashing down when KD started to experience more nightmares, hallucinations, and suicidal thoughts in the first few days of prayers. At first, Emily thought it was a phase that would pass, but as the days went by, it became apparent that KD was battling with something far more significant than a phase.

KD's nightmares were so vivid that he would wake up in the middle of the night screaming and sweating, describing monsters and demons chasing after him.

When KD revealed all that he was going through in a very long conversation with Emily, she tried to calm him down and reassure him that it was only a bad dream which could be handled spiritually by her pastor. KD was convinced it was more than that. He felt that something had taken possession of his life and was controlling his thoughts and actions because of the initiation and sacrifices he had been through. He suspected it must be the cult members or the chief priest who are trying to get at him. He knew if he didn't return to them with the final big sacrifice, they would come after him through whatever means possible.

On several occasions, KD would experience hallucinations and see things that were not really there. He would talk to imaginary people and go into a trance-like state, where he was unresponsive to Emily's calls. It was a challenging period for Emily as she watched her boyfriend's mental health spiral out of control. To make matters worse, KD started to have more suicidal thoughts again and would talk about how life was meaningless, and he felt like he was a burden to all members of his family and Emily.

Emily was devastated by KD's condition, and she felt initially helpless. She could not bear to see the man she loved so much lose himself to these demons. However, Emily was a woman of faith, and she knew that God was the ultimate deliverer and healer. She began to pray fervently, asking God to give her the strength to join with her pastor and stand in the gap, and help KD overcome his demons.

At first, KD was sceptical of Emily's prayers and did not fully believe. He felt that his condition was beyond redemption and that he would be stuck in that state forever until the Occult grandmaster kills him. However, as Emily continued to pray and stand in the gap for him, KD started to notice a change in his perspective. He felt more positive and hopeful, and he started to believe that God had not abandoned him. This made him submit fully to the deliverance ministration prayers.

THE BATTLES

The battles were many and intense. If they were to be recorded, a big book could be written on this topic alone.

This little recording was based on an agreement. The agreement was between KD and Emily's pastor. It was agreed that the issue of deliverance be kept confidential. It was agreed that only the inner circle, comprising the pastor, Emily and himself, would know and preserve all the details of the deliverance ministration.

The actual battle with the demonic forces lasted for over two weeks. The first week was spent by Emily and her pastors laying the foundation for the deliverance ministrations. That was when it looked like things were getting worse.

All memorabilia and items of satanic worship were all returned to the church for burning.

There was a rededication of KD's life and beliefs to Jesus Christ. There was a renouncing of the Absalom god and the marine spirits. All the covenants with the Devil and the Marine world were broken. All curses were broken. All spiritual plants of the enemy were uprooted.

Spiritual warehouses were demolished and there was no stone left untouched. Everywhere KD's photographs or articles were used for diabolical purposes, came under fire.

Even though Emily and her pastors were working by faith, there was a confirmation from a phone call made by an ex-cult member to Silas, saying there had been physical fire incidents at the cult center. Hope was rising all the time.

Emily started to take KD to church with her, and they would attend extra deliverance prayer meetings in the evenings, during midweek fellowships. KD began to see that he was not alone in his struggles, and that other people had overcome similar challenges by faith through Jesus Christ.

Emily's faith was contagious, and soon enough, KD started to pray and minister deliverance for himself. He would spend hours reading the Bible and meditating on God's promises. As the weeks went by, KD's nightmares and hallucinations reduced significantly, and he felt more in control of his life. Emily and KD were overjoyed at God's grace and love, and they felt like they had a new lease on life.

KD's suicidal thoughts also vanished, and he began to see that his life was valuable and meaningful. He started to appreciate the love and support that Emily and the Church had shown him, and he felt like he had a purpose in life.

KD started to see a therapist in Emily's church who helped him work through his emotions and thoughts. The therapist was amazed at KD's progress and could not believe how much he had improved. KD's recovery was a miracle to many, and it was evident that the power of God had played a significant part in his healing.

Today, KD is back on his feet, and he and Emily are happier than ever. They continue to pray together and support each other through life's ups and downs. KD is now a beacon of hope to others who are struggling with mental health challenges, and he draws strength from his faith in God.

Emily's story is a testament to the power of prayer and the miracles that God can perform. It is also a reminder that mental health challenges do not have to be battled alone, and that with the right support and faith, one can overcome any obstacle. Emily's unwavering faith and love for KD, proved that true love can conquer all, and they are a living testament to this fact.

Chapter Eleven

The Victory

After over two weeks of intense spiritual battles, the attacks on KD finally subsided. He no longer had nightmares or physical symptoms, and he felt like himself again. Emily and KD were both relieved and grateful for the help they had received from the Church.

They knew that the battle was far from over, but they were confident that they could handle anything that came their way. They continued to practice their spiritual beliefs and daily prayers, knowing that they were the key to protecting themselves from the dark forces that had threatened their relationship.

MAINTAINING THE VICTORY

The real battle was fighting to maintain the victory. When devils are driven away from their comfort zone, they will still come back to see if they can inhabit the same place again.

The first sign of victory was the withdrawal by the devil, of everything physical that the devil's agents had given KD, including properties, cars and cash. There were mishaps after mishaps leading to loss of properties and cash.
When the devil was leaving the place, he packed his properties and left hoping to return another time.

To ensure the devils did not return, KD had to be intentional about maintaining his body, soul and spirit. He had to watch what he did with his eyes, his ears and mind. He had to watch what we did with his body, soul and spirit.

STUDYING THE BIBLE.

KD spent ample time studying the Bible every day. He discovered that the only way to get close to God, was to get the word of God inside his spirit man every day. Just like he will eat physical food three times a day, he now eats spiritual food by studying the Holy Bible. He began to discover several hidden truths about the positive supernatural. After tasting the negative, he now knows the difference. He even discovered that he could pray effectively and effectually using the Holy bible.

HOLY SPIRIT

Partnership with the Holy Spirit was something he understood and implemented initially. He had been used to the spirit world. Although he had renounced the demon gods that worked for him while in the occult church, he found it difficult to resist them at the end of the year, when he wanted favours. What did he do when he wanted favours? It was like dog returning to its vomit. This will be laid bare in the next series.

TRANSFORMATION

He understood what God meant when He instructed through the Holy Spirit that we should not be conformed to this world. He instructed expressly that we should not be conformed to this world, but be transformed by the renewing of our mind, that we may prove what is that good and acceptable and perfect will of God.

He also understood what God meant when he instructed that we grieve not the Holy Spirit. He knew that he needed to do away with envy, bitterness and evil speaking. Unfortunately this was a hard task for KD. From time to time, he would go on the social media and start ranting about his past dealings with men of God. He would even lay a curse openly on any man of God who parades himself as a healer and yet cannot heal people suffering during a pandemic. Out of the same mouth that released blessings earlier in the day, oozed curses at night and swear words even at men of God.

MAMMON

His short lived affluence and flirtation with mammon was too sweet to forget.

Even after the devil had collected back most of what KD received as an occult prophet, he still had a lot to enjoy after his deliverance.

He knew his threshold of enjoyment. Anything below this, he would find a way to connect with his favourite occult prophets to make illicit money. This money would never last as it goes straight into private parties and reveling without the knowledge or consent of Emily. It was difficult for him to stop serving Mammon. Opening doors to Mammon was an area that made it hard for KD to maintain his deliverance. How did he conquer mammon? Details of this will be in the next series.

DISCIPLINE

The discipline to study the positive supernatural and obey kingdom principles, was a huge task for KD. This was one of his biggest challenges. Not knowing the kingdom principles and inability to follow the little he knew, made it hard for him to conform.

The Devil encouraged KD to live in the flesh rather than in the Spirit. He spent half his time chasing worldly pleasures. Even after reconciling with Emily, he still went after his old friends for occasional worldly parties.

He allowed himself to dwell in the past, rather than moving on. Because he is a good thinker, he allowed himself to ruminate on his past journeys. He apportioned blames on his "spiritual fathers", rather than on himself for his past failures. He sank more into the sin of no forgiveness. This he did by refusing to forgive, and holding on to offences against him from other men of God. It led to the development of the root of bitterness, which was hard to deal with in later years as we will find out very soon in the next series. At some point, he had to go on social media to vent his anger on men of God, to draw sympathy from members of the public. Drawing sympathy from the public was one thing, but dividing the body of Christ was the ultimate goal. He was aiding division wherever he was allowed to do so, weakening the witness of the church and its ability to impact the world with the gospel of Jesus Christ.

To maintain deliverance and stay free from demons, KD was instructed to deny self and consecrate himself so he will be more useful to the Kingdom of God. This was a herculean task, as he found himself placing more focus on self instead of denying self, to love, serve and be a blessing to the body of Christ.

It must be remembered that it was the selfishness of KD that led him to seek occult powers so he could be richer than his spiritual fathers. He encouraged selfishness rather than giving generously of his substance.

Even after the deliverance, KD was still drawn to his feelings rather than to his faith in the word of God. He was still an advocate or champion of "seeing is believing". He knew how to flaunt his little wealth and the two remaining cars which the Devil left behind for him, hoping to come back another time. KD was focusing more on feelings and circumstances, rather than on faith in the Word.

At this stage, one would expect that the young man understood how to work with the Holy Spirit, and not depend on self or natural abilities. Unfortunately he was still relying on his connections and physical strength. He must have forgotten about the scripture which says that; "By strength shall no man prevail".

Developing an apathy to church fellowships was rebellious to say the least. The young man once campaigned that people do not have to go to church to be blessed. He was then fostering independent and rebellious attitudes, encouraging Christians to ignore fellowships, contrary to Kingdom principles. But all these he was doing because he wanted more people to leave the churches and follow him online.

Chapter Twelve

The Aftermath

Emily and KD's relationship grew stronger through the spiritual battle they fought together. They both gained a new appreciation for the power of positive energy and the importance of protecting themselves from negative influences.

They continued to practice their spiritual beliefs, not only for their own protection but also to help others who were struggling with similar issues. They knew that their experience could be a source of strength and inspiration for others, and they were committed to sharing their story with anyone who needed to hear it.

With the help of Emily's pastor, they both started their individual Online Ministries and became famous on social media.

Whereas the ministry of KD was based on reconciling himself to the body of Christ and reconciling other men and women of God who have gone astray back to the body of Christ, the ministry of Emily was based on support for women involved in missions inside and outside the country.

Because of the bad tastes left in his mouth from the bad experience of the occult church, KD swore never to go back into church business again. This is because the church business made him notorious for the bad things.

Once in a while to make ends meet, he took up some prophetic engagements as guest minister in other churches. Although he had renounced the demon gods that worked for him while in the occult church, he found it difficult to resist them when the engagements came calling. This was more like the dog returning to its vomit. He didn't know that all these were opening doors for the devil to come in and attack again. And when the devil does come, he comes with stronger demons. We will see how he managed this in the next series.

Chapter Thirteen

Lessons from the Author

This book goes to the root of familiar mental health issues plaguing young adults today. It delves into a case of severe depression, phobias, and attempted suicide which nearly ruined a promising young man of God.

Many lessons can be learnt from this true-life story. A few of them stand out, considering that in this fiction, the actors had to choose between life and death. Let's look at some of the lessons.

The counterfeit rule

The first lesson I want to share is the counterfeit rule. Have you noticed that in life, when blessings are approaching you in the form of answers to prayers, the enemy is quick to provide a counterfeit before the original arrives. The idea is to distract you from the original. Whether it is a business deal, employment, a spouse, or even a home, counterfeits usually surface first. When it comes to the Power of God, there are many vendors of negative supernatural powers, readily available and harder working to sell you their counterfeit powers. Many will even follow you on social media and will bombard you with messages suggesting that they do not have anything to do with human sacrifice and that their power is genuine. This is one way that the devil deceives many into accepting counterfeits, and therefore lose sight of the original. Of course, we know that the devil's main job description is to delay, steal, kill, and destroy original blessings. This is one way he does it. One must never be in a hurry to accept such offers. Just remind yourself that the God of originality is still alive and well. He will always answer with the original blessings and not the quick counterfeits that won't stand the test of time.

Inordinate ambition of some young ones

One good lesson is about the relationship between age and dreams. There is nothing wrong with having big dreams as a teenager or young person, but you must be sure you are not being driven by hormones or lured by the devil to do the wrong things. In the recent past, some young people have committed all kinds of fraud, scams, ritual kidnappings, banditry, and murder, all in the name of getting rich quickly. This has dented the image of Africans both at home and abroad. This get rich quick syndrome is not only confined to Africa. It is now found all over the world, and Satan the devil is capitalizing on it to destroy both the young and old ones.

Envy towards elders, mentors and fathers
Another clear lesson is the danger of envy, especially envy towards mentors and fathers. Whether it's a biological father or a spiritual father, once envy sets in, the devil sees an open door to attack. Why open the door to the devil when you can open the same door of your heart to the original blessings from our Lord Jesus Christ.

Root of Bitterness
Bitterness can be a killer too. You might be someone trusted to give advice to a superior or vise versa. If you allow the root of

bitterness to develop, you are surely opening the door for the devil. Ahithophel was a trusted adviser to King David, but owing to the root of bitterness developing, Ahithophel betrayed the King and joined forces with Absalom. He finally ended his life tragically by committing suicide. II Samuel☐ 17:23☐ NKJV☐☐ "Now when Ahithophel saw that his advice was not followed, he saddled a donkey, and arose and went home to his house, to his city. Then he put his household in order, and hanged himself, and died; and he was buried in his father's tomb."

Once you are able to resist the demons of pride, anger, envy bitterness and their associates, you make it impossible for the devils Absalom, Ahithophel and their cohorts to pop a champagne against you.

Praying partners

One of the objectives for writing this true life fiction is to encourage praying partners. Whether married or unmarried, one should be able to watch and pray for the other. Whether your partner is a big man or woman of God, you must stand in the gap on a regular basis because we are not ignorant of the devices of the devil. The bigger your partner in terms of fame and wealth, the more the prayers. God Himself saw well in advance what will happen to your partner. This is why He sent you to stand in the gap and save him or her. Just imagine this instruction in Jude chapter 1 verse 23: "save others by snatching them from the fire; to others show mercy, mixed with fear—hating even the clothing stained by corrupted flesh".

Test the spirits

One very good lesson that cannot be glanced over is the testing of the spirits. The scriptures encouraged us to test the spirits. "Dear friends, do not believe every spirit, but test the spirits to see whether they are from God because many false prophets have gone out into the world." 1 John 4:1 NIV. There are various ways to prayerfully test the spirits. Some of the ways are explained in 1 John chapter 4.

Gratitude to God

I will explain the next lesson as it relates to the 80/20 per cent rule. Most couples complain or whinge when they recognize their partner has 80% of the qualities they desire, while lacking in the balance 20%. They are then quick to complain and focus on the 20% rather than be grateful to God for the 80%. This is one area that opens the door for the devil to come in. The devil will magnify the 20% and look for all avenues to destroy the partnership. The devil in the life of KD was busy magnifying this 20%, but Emily remained resolute and unshaken throughout, becoming even more prayerful.

Recognising the devil behind

The next lesson is about recognising the devil behind the partner. In this book, I have tried to shift the focus away from the players. The need to focus on what is behind the partner can not be overemphasized. This has led me to coin my favourite word: "Locate the devil to dislocate the devil." Emily knew there was something behind her partner, so she directed her arsenal towards the devil.

Perseverance definitely pays

It paid off for Emily. We were instructed by the Holy Scriptures to persevere. "Blessed is the one who perseveres under trial because, having stood the test, that person will receive the crown of life that the Lord has promised to those who love him." James 1:12 NIV. It is essential that when we are helping out our partners or friends or relatives in prayer, we persevere. The victim should be taught and encouraged to forgive himself or herself until final resolution, complete deliverance, and healing is achieved.

The Devil's key assignments

There are certain devils that work, not just to delay, to steal, or to destroy. They are bent on killing. So it is with the spirit of Absalom. His ultimate goal is to kill. We must, therefore, watch out for the spirit of suicide. When this devil is dealing with his prey, he does not think anything else but murder.

Deliverance is free for everyone

We can learn from this episode, that deliverance can come to whoever is ready to receive it for free anywhere. To receive deliverance, one must create the atmosphere for the miracle. The difference is in the atmosphere. The condition for the Lord God to send down his power, not forsaking the getting together with other Christians.
Hebrews☐ 10:25☐ NKJV☐☐ "not forsaking the assembling of ourselves together, as is the manner of some, but exhorting one another..." However as the saying goes, it is not what we do when we gather that really matters. It is what we do when we scatter.

The Danger of Pursuing Power the Wrong Way

The protagonist, Prophet KD, falls into severe depression and faces various challenges as a result of his pursuit of power and fame in the wrong manner. This serves as a cautionary tale about the consequences of seeking power through negative means.

Importance of Seeking Help and Support

Prophet KD's struggles highlight the importance of seeking help and support when facing mental health issues, spiritual battles, and challenges. Silas, as a supportive friend, encourages KD to discuss his problems and seek guidance from his loved ones.

The Power of Prayer and Faith

The unwavering faith and prayers of Emily, the woman in KD's life, played a crucial role in his redemption and recovery. This underscores the transformative power of prayer and belief in overcoming obstacles and spiritual battles.

Communication and Transparency in Relationships

Silas encourages KD to consider opening up to Emily and discussing his struggles with her. This emphasizes the importance of communication and transparency in relationships, as well as the value of seeking support from loved ones during difficult times.

Resilience and Overcoming Adversity

Despite facing overwhelming challenges and being on the brink of despair, there is a sense of resilience and determination in KD's journey towards redemption. This portrays the strength of the human spirit in overcoming adversity and finding a way forward.

Practical Christianity

Practical and Biblical Solutions for Mental Health issues can be helpful. That the author offered practical and biblical solutions at the end of some chapters, to help individuals facing similar challenges and to prevent such situations from occurring in the future, speaks to the importance of integrating spiritual and practical approaches in addressing mental health issues.

Overall, "Saving Him from Absalom" explores themes of power, faith, love, mental health, and redemption, offering valuable insights and lessons on navigating spiritual battles and personal struggles.

In conclusion, as I usually say, God might have intentionally planted you in your family for such a time as this. After reading this book, you could be helping to save somebody in your family. You could be helping to save your friends and relatives.

In your action plan, please use the blank pages provided at the end of this book to make some personal notes. May God use you to execute his plans and purposes on earth.

PERSONAL NOTES

PERSONAL NOTES

PERSONAL NOTES

PERSONAL NOTES

ABOUT THE AUTHOR

Rockson Rapu is a British polymer scientist and business consultant, born into a family of men and women of God from Nigeria. He was called over three decades ago, and the gracious hand of the Lord Almighty was upon his life and led him to excel as an entrepreneur and mentor to the next generation. He is an ordained minister and has served in a variety of mentorship roles. This has helped him to understand and relate to the things that people are going through in these end-times. He is the award-winning author of – SAVING HER FROM JEZEBEL.

Rockson Rapu is married and blessed with three God-fearing and diligent daughters and many spiritual sons and daughters, by whom he has been inspired to share so much wisdom through this novel.

Printed in Great Britain
by Amazon